Michelle

And Daniel

own Tales

ERNEST AR...

This edition ©Ward Lock Limited 1989

First published in the United States
in 1990 by Gallery Books,
an imprint of W.H. Smith Publishers, Inc.,
112 Madison Avenue, New York 10016.

Gallery Books are available for bulk purchase for sales
promotions and premium use. For details write or telephone
the Manager of Special Sales, W.H. Smith Publishers, Inc.,
112 Madison Avenue, New York, New York 10016. (212) 532-6600.

ISBN 0-8317-0972-3

Printed and bound in Hungary

THE BRAMBLEDOWN TALES

HOPPITY HARE'S ADVENTURES

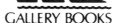

GALLERY BOOKS

An Imprint of W. H. Smith Publishers Inc
112 Madison Avenue
New York, New York 10016

Off to market

Chapter One

A WONDERFUL SHOP

On the other side of the river, but before you come to the sea, lies the village of Brambledown. Do you know it? If you are up and about early enough, and you listen very carefully, you might hear a strange rustling and scampering and wiffling and scuffling and pattering and trundling and whispering. It is coming from the hill above Farmer Hayseed's garden. But it isn't Farmer Hayseed. He's still in bed. He wouldn't like it if he knew what it really was.

You see, it is the sound of birds and animals from all over Brambledown. They are off to market to do their shopping. And do you know where they go to market? In Farmer Hayseed's back garden. There's always plenty of food if you know where to look!

Down from the barns and over from the farmyard and out of the wood and off the fields they used to come – the Brown Rabbit family and the Field-Mouse family and Henry the Hedgehog and Ronnie Rook, a squadron of starlings, a skirl of squirrels, a sprinkling of snails and a handful of hens. Maurice the Mole and a whole treeful of assorted birds. And just sometimes, Hoppity Hare would come too.

Henry Hedgehog

In through the gate or over the fence, the long procession came to collect their day's groceries . . . because the garden is full of wonderful things!

There are turnips, lettuces, cabbages and parsley, carrots and broccoli, marrows, sprouts, peas and beans, tomatoes, kale, beetroot and spinach, rhubarb and celery.

Everybody ate a big breakfast and chatted, telling each other their news and choosing the best and the biggest produce. Then it was back to the hill or the wood or the farmyard or the fields, carrying as much food as two paws or a beak could hold.

Some would eat so much breakfast that they had to stop for a snooze on the way home. But most were glad to get the day's shopping home to their hungry children.

"What a wonderful shop it is!" they all agreed. "How kind of Farmer Hayseed to open it for us." But then they giggled, because they knew full well how angry poor Farmer Hayseed felt about the birds and animals who dug up his garden every morning. If ever he came out into the garden, they quickly scurried away and hid. But, of course, when he went back inside his cottage, it was safe to come out again.

And one day last summer something happened to change everything.

Mrs Mouse saw the start of it.

Mrs Mouse has a particularly large and hungry family. And although she had been to the garden-market once in the morning, with the other animals, by evening there was not a bite left.

Mrs Mouse saw the start

So off she pattered, down the lane. She squeezed between the bars of the little blue gate and began to choose her groceries. "A little bit of this, I think. And a little bit of that. A taste of these and a bite of . . . oh!" A loud noise made her whiskers tremble and she quickly bolted behind the bean-poles to hide.

Out of the farm cottage came Farmer Hayseed – a hundred times higher than a mouse, in his Wellington boots and flapping coat. He had his arm round another human – someone just as big and frightening, and wearing the same sort of flapping coat.

Now it wasn't the first time that Farmer Hayseed had come out into the garden and frightened away a little creature shopping late in his vegetable patch.

Mrs Mouse had heard the door bang before. She had felt the ground tremble as he tramped down the path. She had smelled the strange smell and trembled at the great size of the human giant. She had seen him plant tasty young lettuces and pick some beans for his wife. He always left plenty for the animals when he went stamping back into the house. And, when they heard his door slam, they knew it was safe to come out again.

But Mrs Mouse had never seen his friend before. And there was something much more terrible about the second giant. When Farmer Hayseed stamped back down the garden path and went inside for his supper, his tall, ugly giant of a friend stayed out in the garden. He stayed and he stood and he stared straight ahead.

"Go and see for yourselves"

Chapter Two

THE TERRIBLE STRANGER

"It was terrible!" cried Mrs Mouse. "I waited half the night for him to go. But he just stayed and he stood and he stared! He's there now, just standing and staring!"

"You mistook."

"It was very late."

"You were tired."

"It's nothing, Mrs Mouse."

"Oh do come along. It's time for market." said Maurice Mole impatiently. "We all know that Mrs Mouse is a very *nervous* kind of person. She is easily scared."

Mrs Mouse put her basket on the ground and sat on it. "Go and see for yourselves if you don't believe me! *I'm* not going back there. Not until the giant has gone. I'll stay here where it's safe."

"Who's going to go to market?"

The animals and birds of Brambledown all looked at one another. Some were still drowsy with sleep. Some were shivering in the early morning cold.

"Easy-peasy! I'll go!" declared Timmy the tiniest Mouse.

"You'll do no such thing!" said his mother, grabbing his collar.

"Will too! Will too! I'm not afraid of nothing!" And off ran the disobedient little Mouse, boasting, "I'm brave, I am! I don't care at all about any giant!"

In a few moments he came back again. His tail was stiff and his ears were limp. His nose was pale and his paws were trembling.

"It's an 'orrible ogre!" he whispered. "It's a terrible troll! It's a monstrous big monster. It's a great . . . big . . .

GIANT!"

"Easy-peasy! I'll go!"

"Shame on you, Timmy Mouse," said Mrs Brown. "Don't tell lies. Don't you know it's wicked to try and frighten people?" And nobody believed Timmy the tiniest Mouse – except for Mrs Mouse, of course – because he liked to tell lies and make up stories and pretend to be very brave.

Timmy told lies

Even so, none of the animals very much wanted to go and look in the garden to prove that there was no 'orrible ogre or terrible troll or monstrous monster.

"Why doesn't somebody fly over the garden?" suggested Henry Hedgehog, and the little creatures of Brambledown quickly agreed it was a good idea. After all, they were beginning to get very hungry for their breakfasts. (Henry thought it was a particularly good idea, because hedgehogs can't fly, so he would not have to go.)

"I'll do it," said Ronnie Rook. "Wait here!" And he thought to himself, "Now I can pick out the best things in the garden for myself, before the others arrive." He spread his black wings and flapped away towards the garden-market. Soon he was just a small black speck

"Wait here!"

in the distance. The black speck flew in a big circle over the farm cottage. Then it hovered over the spot where the giant stood.

Back came Ronnie Rook, flapping his wings fast and furious. His beak gaped wide and he made a most odd noise: "Awk! Awk! It's horrible! It's terrible! It's dreadful! It's ghastly! It's AWK-ful!"

"I told you so, but you wouldn't listen," said Timmy Mouse smugly, and his mother gave him a smack for being rude.

"So. The giant is still there. Just as I told you," said Mrs Mouse.

"He just stays and stands and stares," gasped Ronnie Rook. His small black eyes shone with terror. "A horrible human. A monstrous man!"

"This is getting serious," said Barney Brown (who was starting to feel *very* hungry for his breakfast.) "Why don't we all go together and see this horrible human, this monstrous man? There's no need to be afraid if we all go together. Together we can be brave as brave! Together we can face anything!"

And with this stirring cry, he lifted one paw in the air and led the way down the lane towards Farmer Hayseed's garden. The animals followed close behind.

As they got closer to the little blue gate, Barney Brown rabbit slowed down. All the other animals straggling out behind him bumped into one another. Somehow, Henry Hedgehog ended up in front.

The timid creatures hung back. The bravest stood on tiptoe and tried to see over the fence without being seen.

"*Shshsh!*" hissed Maurice Mole and everybody jumped half out of their skins.

"*Shshshsh!*" they hissed back at him, and soon everybody was hissing and shushing and shushing and hissing and putting their paws to their lips.

One by one they crept forward and peeped through the bars of the little blue gate. What they saw made their fur (or feathers) stand on end and their mouths drop open and their hearts thud.

"I've never seen the like!"

"It's horrible."

"It's terrible."

"It's ghastly."

It's awful."

"It's scarey."

"It's BIG!"

"*We can never come here again.*"

"Not while he's standing there watching for us," said Henry Hedgehog. "If he sees us, will he chase us and eat us?" But when Henry looked round for an answer, there was nobody there. All the others were running as fast as their legs would carry them – back up the lane. They fell over their own paws. They fell over each other. Mrs Brown bundled her family into a barrow and ran and ran and ran.

And ran and ran and ran

"I say! What the . . . ? Look out!. . . Oof!"

Chapter Three

HOPPITY HEARS THE NEWS

Helter-skelter, the little shoppers of Brambledown fled. They were quite sure the giant in the garden would see them and come after them to gobble them down, fur and feather, paws and claws.

They did not see Hoppity Hare coming towards them. They did not see him raise his stick in the air and greet them with a cheery, "Good morning." In their panic they ran straight at him, straight into him, straight over him, shouting, "Shop's shut! Shop's shut! Giant on the loose! Make way! Watch out!"

"I say! What the . . ? Look out! . . . Oof!" Poor Hoppity was bowled head-over-heels and trampled by a great variety of bird claws and animal paws.

"Hoppity-woppity!" cried Hoppity lying on his back looking up at the sky. "I've been run over! That wasn't very friendly! Hoppity-woppity! And on such a nice morning, too! Would somebody tell me what's going on? Did I say something? Did I do something to annoy? Or is it a new game? Hare-rushing? Hare-brushing? I

"Not very friendly"

don't like it! I have to tell you I don't like the game one bit!"

But there was nobody to answer him.

Hoppity Hare picked himself up very slowly and carefully. He looked to left and right (just in case they were coming back again at the gallop). He shook the dust out of his ears and out of his tail. And the more he dusted, the more angry he got.

At last, he put up his fists like a boxer and exclaimed, "Hoppity-woppity! Come back and I'll fight you one by one! Just see if I won't!"

Now I don't know if you realize, but hares can be very fierce indeed, with their quick-punching paws and their long, kicking feet. And no hare is fiercer than Hoppity. There was not an animal in Brambledown who would purposely upset Hoppity Hare, for he has a punch like lightning and a way of kicking naughty youngsters all the way from here Monday through to Friday. And to tell you the truth, he does have rather a fiery temper, too.

When he heard running footsteps coming along the lane, he danced about in a fearful rage, and he thought to himself, "Here comes another one who wants to run me over! I'd better stay out of the way."

Coming down the lane from Farmer Hayseed's garden was Henry Hedgehog, puffing and panting as he ran.

Hoppity hid

Hoppity hid in the bushes, muttering and mumbling angrily. Along came Henry, running as fast as he knew how. With his little, short legs, he could not keep up with the other animals.

"Wait for me! Don't leave me behind to be eaten!" he panted. "Make way for Henry!"

"Hoppity-woppity!" cried Hoppity leaping out of the bush, his paws tucked up in front of his chest. "What's the meaning of it?"

At the sight of Hoppity, Henry rolled himself up into a trembling, prickly ball.

"I suppose you wanted to run me over, too!" shouted Hoppity in his ear.

"Come out and explain yourself!" bellowed Hoppity. But Henry kept silent.

"Hoppity-woppity, I'm getting really mad!" and he gave Henry a sharp kick.

Well, it was a sharp kick for Hoppity: sharp and bristly and painful. "*Owowowow!*"

Henry unrolled himself at last to watch Hoppity hopping about. "It serves you right. You shouldn't try to stop me escaping from the terrible troll."

"The what?"

"The 'orrible ogre."

"The who?"

"The monstrous man. The ghastly giant!"

"Hoppity-woppity! What is this nonsense?"

So Henry explained about the horrible human. As he listened, Hoppity's brown eyes grew wider and rounder and rounder and wider.

Finally Henry said, "So you see, we must all run away and hide. I only hope it won't eat too many of us!" And he turned to run away.

Turned to run

"Stay right where you are!"

Chapter Four

HOPPITY SEES FOR HIMSELF

"Hold on now! Stay right where you are, Henry Hedgehog!" cried Hoppity fiercely. "Hoppity-woppity! I never heard such nonsense in my life! Where is this monstrous man? Show me this instant! I have to see him with my own eyes."

"He's in Farmer Hayseed's garden," said Henry Hedgehog. "You don't need me to show you the way there. I'm *never* going back. Nobody is ever going back. Not while the giant stays standing there, staring. You might be brave, Mr Hare, but even *you* won't be going to market in Farmer Hayseed's garden again! Not after you've seen the giant with your very own eyes."

"We'll just see about that," said Hoppity.

So off he went to see the monster for himself.

Henry snuffled and snorted (as hedgehogs do) and went on his way as fast as his short legs would carry him. But he kept looking back over his shoulder.

"There he goes. Just wait till he sees it. He'll be just as scared as me when he sees it. Just see if he won't. He's so rash and reckless, that hare. People say he's quite mad. Well, let him go! The giant will probably eat him up and spit out his ears. The giant will probably grab him and skin him and cook him and . . . owowow! Poor, dear Hoppity! Come back, Hoppity! Please don't go near the garden any more!"

And the more Henry thought, the more he worried about Hoppity. His run slowed down to a walk. His walk slowed down to a crawl. Then he stopped. Then he turned round and crept slowly, slowly, back the way he had come.

Meanwhile, Hoppity Hare reached the garden. He crept up to the little blue gate on his long brown feet, and he peeped through the bars.

Inside him, his heart leaped as high as a hare. The story was true! There stood the giant in a horrible hat. Two long arms stretched out wide, as if he wanted to wrap Hoppity in his arms and hug him to pieces. The giant had a long, flapping coat and two staring silver eyes and a pipe and . . . *one wooden leg.*

And he stood and he stared and he stayed staring, and the sun made his eyes dazzle and the wind made his coat flap. He was ten times taller than Hoppity.

A little voice said in Hoppity's ear, "Didn't I tell you so?" It was Henry Hedgehog.

"Didn't I tell you?"

All the way home, they talked about the giant.

"Hoppity-woppity! Something must be done!"

Henry nodded sadly. "Yes, yes. We must find somewhere else to go shopping."

"Hoppity-woppity! Where's your courage?"

"I think I left it at home," said Henry. "I don't care if people think I'm a coward. I never wanted to be a hero."

"Nor me," said Hoppity, and he almost patted Henry on the back, but he remembered all the spines.

"I know!" said Henry. "Let's have a meeting to discuss the problem."

"Must we?" said Hoppity.

"Let's have a meeting!"

You see, usually, when the animals of Brambledown have a problem, they ask Hoppity. They climb the hill to the door of his burrow, and they ask him, because he always gives such wise answers.

But Hoppity could not find any wise answers in his head that day. His heart was still pounding, his ears were still quivering. For a fine, fierce hare, he felt very foolish and afraid.

At the meeting Maurice Mole said, "I suppose we must go exploring for another market. Isn't that right, Hoppity?"

Barney Brown said, "Obviously we must all eat less. Isn't that right, Hoppity?"

Mrs Chick the hen said, "No, no. We must simply dash into the garden and dash out again. Isn't that right, Hoppity? How fast can the giant chase us on one wooden leg?"

"And when winter comes, the giant will go inside out of the cold. Isn't that right, Hoppity?" said Ronnie Rook.

"I don't know," said Hoppity. "Sorry."

"Well! That's a lot of help!"

"Well! And we thought you were supposed to be wise!"

So Hoppity crept away and stood behind a fence-post and said nothing at all. He just listened.

The animals squabbled and boasted and quarrelled and argued and bragged:

Hoppity just listened

"Let's find another market."

"Let's move away from Brambledown!"

"Let's drive it out of the garden."

"Let's try to make friends with it."

"Let's all go to sleep and hope it's gone when we wake up." (That was Henry Hedgehog.)

"Let's throw things at it."

"Let's go home and cry."

"Let's kill it!"

Hoppity Hare shook his head sadly. "Hoppity-woppity! What silly animals. They're very good at talking, but I wonder if they will ever decide what to do. So many words and so few brains."

His eyes strayed across the fields. There was Farmer Hayseed on his tractor. There was somebody else in the tractor, too – a big, raggedy man in a horrible hat, with one wooden . . . "Oh my white whiskers!" cried Hoppity.

Farmer Hayseed lifted down the raggedy man and then drove off again, leaving the giant standing right in the middle of the field, arms outstretched and his silver eyes flashing in the sun.

Hoppity sped back to the garden and looked through the bars of the little blue gate. No. The giant still stood there staring, with shining silver eyes. It had not left the market to ride in Farmer Hayseed's tractor. *There was more than one giant!*

Perhaps a whole family of giants had come to live on Farmer Hayseed's land. Perhaps they never went inside out of the cold and rain. Perhaps they never closed their shiny silver eyes. Perhaps they would be all over Brambledown by morning, just staying and standing still and staring, watching out for little animals doing their morning shopping.

Hoppity raced back to the meeting and whispered his news in Henry's ear.

But of course Henry blurted out, "Oh no! Hoppity says that there are *more* giants coming. We won't go marketing again! We shall starve!"

Then with one voice, all the animals turned to Hoppity Hare: "Tell us what to do!"

More than one

Hoppity whispered his news

The March Hare said, "Why ask me?"

"Because you're wise and sensible and brave. Tell us what we must do!"

Hoppity sat very still and thought. In fact he sat so still that everybody thought he had gone to sleep. They were just going to wake him up when he opened his large brown eyes. "It's obvious. We must fight the giant in the garden. Otherwise our childen will go hungry and other giants will come and drive us out of Brambledown."

"Yes-yes-yes-yes-yes!" yapped the little spotted dog, Dick. "Yes-yes-yes-yes! Kill it! Fight it! Who will fight the giant? Who-who-who-who?" Everybody looked at everybody else, waiting for a volunteer.

"Hoppity-woppity! Why, *everybody* must fight it, of course!" declared Hoppity.

"Who? Me?"

Chapter Five

WHO DARES?

"Who? Me?" said Henry.

"You don't mean me?" said Maurice Mole.

"Me? Fight a giant?" clucked Mrs Chick.

"Me? Tackle a troll?" squealed Mrs Mouse.

"Me, with my bad back?" said Barney Brown. And everybody scattered, and ran about bumping into each other, all talking at once, all saying why they could not *possibly* fight the 'orrible ogre.

Hoppity began to say, "Then I suppose it will have to be . . ."

"*I'll go!*" yipped Dick, the spotted dog. "If you'll give me a big reward and call me a hero and make me King of Brambledown, I'll save you from the giant!" He ran round in a circle, chasing his own tail with excitement at the thought of becoming a king.

"Yes, yes. We will give you a reward!"

"Yes, yes. We'll call you a hero, Dick!"

"Yes, yes. You can be King of Brambledown!" All the animals jumped with joy – except wise Hoppity, of course.

Dick gulped

Dick gulped. Suddenly he was not so very brave. But he was a very vain and foolish puppy and he did like the sound of 'Dick, King of Brambledown'. So away he went to Farmer Hayseed's garden to fight the giant. He was so pale with fright that the dark spots on his coat went as white as the rest of him. Step by step, paw by paw, he crept closer to the little blue gate and peeped inside.

The giant glared at him with shining silver eyes and seemed to shake its fist. Dick put his head between the bars of the gate and GROWLED his fiercest growl.

The giant glared and stared and stayed.

Dick opened his throat and he BARKED the biggest and best bark of his life.

But the giant only glared and stared.

Dick bared all his teeth. He hurled himself at the garden gate until its latch rattled and blue paint fell on to his fur.

But the giant only glared and stared and stayed. At last, Dick hurled himself so hard at the gate that it flew open and he found himself standing at the very feet of the giant. The silver eyes seemed to stare right at him.

It was too much for one small puppy to bear. He put his tail between his legs and he RAN all the way back to Brambledown.

When Dick did not come back, the wild creatures said, "He's been eaten by the giant."

But fortunately, Timmy Mouse had gone along to watch the fight and he told them what had really happened.

Timmy told them

There was someone else who watched all the barking and growling and jumping and running, too. Hoppity Hare was so worried about Dick that he went and hid behind the garden fence to see that the little fellow came to no harm. He was so glad to see Dick run away home, safe and sound.

The sun was shining strongly and it cast a long, black shadow against the wall of Hoppity's long ears and sharp-pointed nose. "*Hoppity-woppity!*" the shadow seemed to say. "*Call yourself a hare? Hares are supposed to be brave boxers – ferocious fighters! Hares are supposed to be reckless and rash! Hares are supposed to be fierce and fearless! What are you thinking of, Hoppity? Your friends need you to help them. Brambledown needs you!*"

"Hoppity-woppity! That's good advice, Mr Shadow!" cried Hoppity springing up on to his hind legs and tucking up his paws. "You're absolutely right!" And he threw a few punches at the shadow, just for practice.

He crouched down very low. He laid his long ears flat along his back so that they did not show above the fence. And he crept very, very carefully right round the gar-den until he found

Hoppity hid to watch

an opening *behind* the monstrous man, the horrible human, the big baddie, the terrible troll. His brown paws made not a sound on the soft grass, but every moment he expected the giant to turn and see him . . .

He jumped the fence in a single gigantic bound.

Fists up and punching, balanced on tiptoe and kicking, he gave the loud battle cry:

"*Hoppity is hopping mad!*
Be you big and be you bad!
Put 'em up and fight me, lad!"

He fought ferociously

Chapter Six

HERO HOPPITY!

He surprised the giant from behind, leaping up on to its shoulders. And there he fought ferociously, with teeth and clawed paws and punching and kicking and pulling and tugging and wrestling and roaring:

"Take that! I'll have a go at you! Eat us, would you? Shut our shop, would you? Take that!"

He knocked the pipe out of the giant's mouth. He knocked off the horrible hat. (It fell over his own ears and everything went dreadfully dark until he pushed his head out through the top into the daylight.) He tore the flapping coat from collar to hem.

And every moment he expected the long arms to grab at him and fling him round his hatless head and dash him to the ground.

The giant swayed once, swayed twice and fell on its face. The head rolled away into the turnip patch. After all, it was only a big turnip with bottle-tops for eyes. The long arms went limp and floppy. After all, they were only bundles of straw. The one wooden leg broke with a loud snap. After all, it was only a broomstick. "Hoppity-woppity! You're not a human at all!" snorted the heroic hare. "You're just a bundle of bits put up to frighten us away!" And he scattered the scarecrow all about the garden.

Then he was away over the fence to tell the other animals they had nothing to fear from Farmer Hayseed's home-made giants.

When they heard how they had been tricked, they laughed and cried both at the same time.

A turnip and wisp of straw

Hoppity did not tell them how he knew. You see, Hoppity did not think it was very brave or clever to fight a turnip and a wisp of straw and an old coat.

But fortunately Timmy Mouse had been watching, and he told all Brambledown what had happened. They said Hoppity was a hero. "He thought it was a giant and he still fought it for us. *That's* what counts," said Henry Hedgehog.

But Hoppity only smiled shyly and went back up the hill to watch the sun set. "Hoppity-woppity! What a day it's been!" he said under his breath.

…and an old coat